A *Steve Parish* Story Book

Beautiful Butterfly

To Sam
love from
Vera + Bob
Noosa April 2006

Story by Rebecca Johnson

Photos by Steve Parish

The Ulysses Butterfly was very beautiful.

She loved to show off her brilliant blue wings as she swooped and flittered through the forest.

Everywhere she went,
other insects gazed at her and
told her how pretty she looked.

Unfortunately,
the butterfly had been
told how beautiful
she was so many times,
she began to believe
she was better
than all of the
other insects.

"You are so beautiful," a plain, brown moth called to the butterfly. "I wish I were as pretty as you."

"Oh dear," laughed the butterfly. "I don't think that will happen." And she flew away.

She flew past
a grasshopper
sitting on a flower.
"You look lovely
today," he called.
But she just
ignored him.

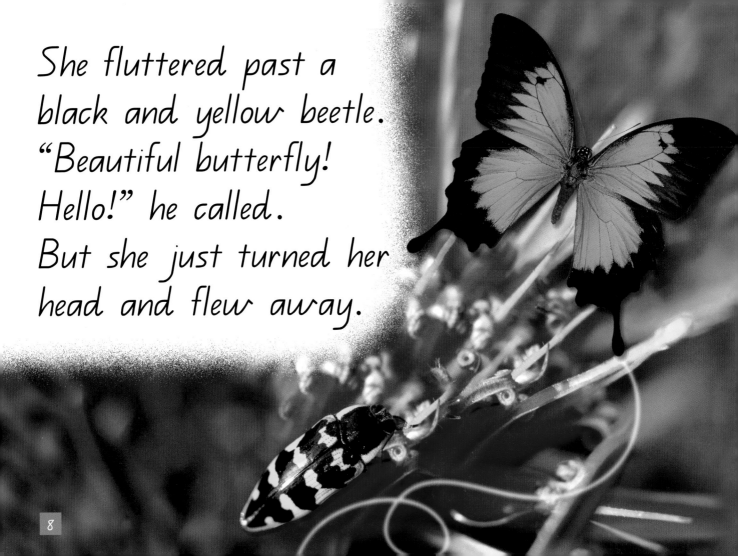

She fluttered past a
black and yellow beetle.
"Beautiful butterfly!
Hello!" he called.
But she just turned her
head and flew away.

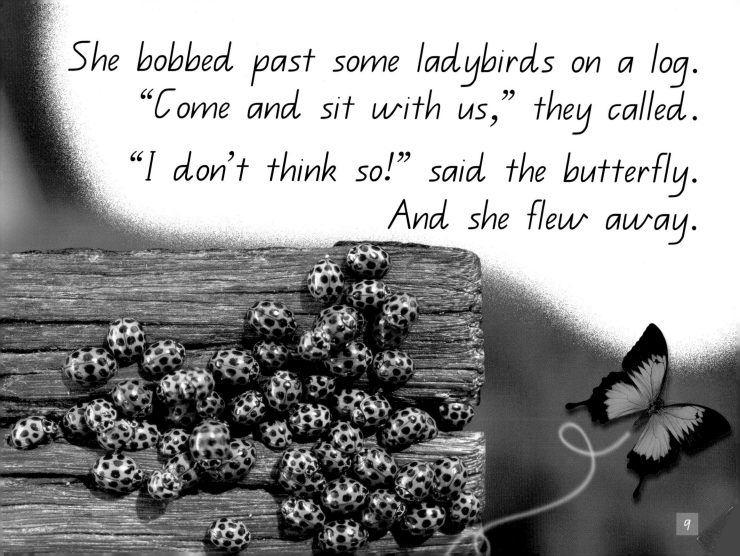

She bobbed past some ladybirds on a log.
"Come and sit with us," they called.

"I don't think so!" said the butterfly.
And she flew away.

She fluttered above a caterpillar sitting on a flower.

"Will I be as beautiful as you one day?" called the caterpillar.

"I doubt it!" laughed the butterfly.

"Oh, it must be awful to be so plain," scoffed the butterfly to a brown beetle. "Even that lovely leaf doesn't brighten you up!"

And so it continued.
The butterfly became
so obsessed
with her own
beauty, she
believed that, unless
you were beautiful,
you were not important.

Then, one day,
a dreadful accident
happened. The butterfly
was flying past a pond,
looking at her reflection
in the water, when she
nearly flew straight into
a large grasshopper.

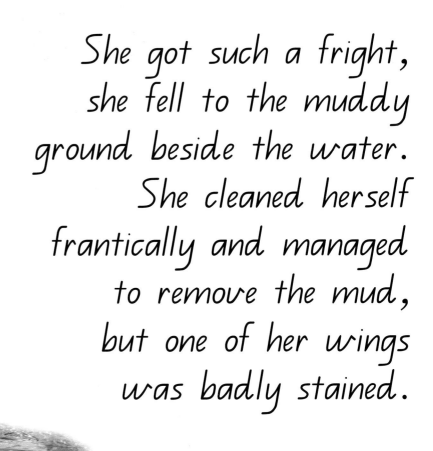

She got such a fright,
she fell to the muddy
ground beside the water.
She cleaned herself
frantically and managed
to remove the mud,
but one of her wings
was badly stained.

"Oh dear!"
cried the
butterfly,
"I am not
beautiful
any more.
I am
worthless."

She hid amongst
some ferns, too
embarrassed to let
the other insects
see how ugly
she had become.

Some time later, a graceful green butterfly landed nearby. The blue butterfly moved deeper into the darkness of the leaves, but the green butterfly saw her.

"Why are you hiding?" he asked.

"I am hiding
because I have
a stain on my wing
and I am ugly,"
she sobbed.

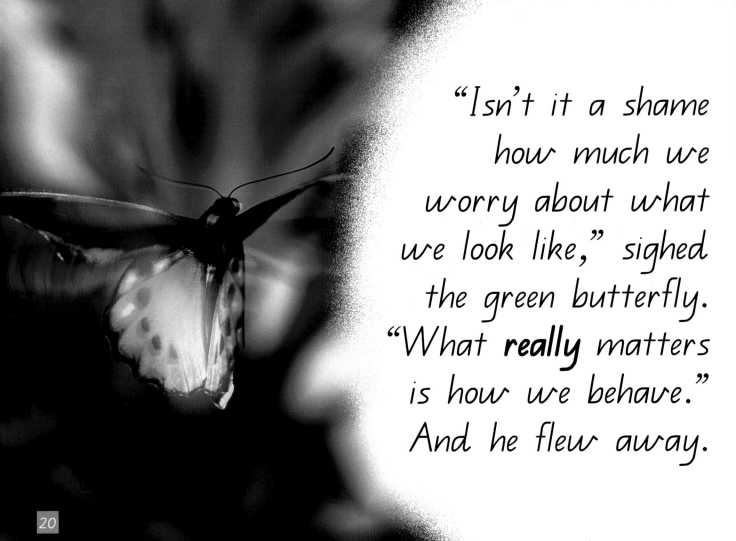

"Isn't it a shame how much we worry about what we look like," sighed the green butterfly. "What **really** matters is how we behave." And he flew away.

The blue butterfly felt so ashamed. She had behaved very badly to all the other insects.

She left her hiding place and flew through the forest, stopping and talking to all kinds of insects. She said she was sorry for being so rude to them.

To her surprise,
they all said
they admired her
far more now
than they had before.